Rosemary's Crush

Nash Nelson

Nash Nelson

This book is a homage to my days of ghostwriting romance stories. I figured I'd give myself a blast from the past this once. I hope you guys enjoy it!

Also, feel free to visit my Patreon page! URL is patreon.com/nashnelson :)

Contents

Rosemary's Crush

1

Another Day In The Office

"Have you ever considered therapy, Rosemary? These delusions are getting out of hand."

Her emerald eyes shimmered under the dull stockroom light. Mania etched itself into the young woman's smile, as it always did when she talked about subjects that ruled her life. She ran her fair hands up and down her sunflower dress. Her excitement was contagious, but only one person in the entire room was sick.

It wasn't Marla, the lowly paid file clerk.

"*Listen to me,*" Rosemary said, raising her voice. "There is evidence that the government is hiding something big at Area 51. What is it? We already know they're researching the overlords of the sky! Why keep *this* a secret? Why the lack of transparency?"

Marla stood on her tiptoes, her curly black hair bouncing when she landed back on the pads of her feet. "And I suppose a stockroom girl is going to unveil the truth?"

Rosemary laughed loudly, her wild eyes widening to unhinged proportions. "Honey, I've *been* unveiling the truth for years now. Don't knock someone because they stock shelves and clean out paper shredders for a living!"

The file clerk rolled her eyes and turned back to sort through a box full of outdated contracts. "Whatever, Rosemary. You keep saying shit like that and you're gonna get Baker-Acted one of these days."

The strawberry blonde blew a raspberry from her lips. "*Please.* Last time I was Baker-Acted, all they did was give me meds that made me sleep," Rosemary ran a hand through her hair, fingertips caressing the brown roots that were growing out. "I don't need sleep, Marla. I need to be awake and spread the word of the mothers and fathers of our very existence!"

Marla shook her head. "I'm really busy. Get back to doing your *own* job before I report you for harassment."

Rosemary scoffed, dramatically turning around to leave the stockroom. "Whatever. You'll thank me one of these days."

As the woman stormed out of the room, she stomped through the office floor in her stiletto heels. The cubicle monkeys click-clacked on their keyboards, sipping their coffee as she walked by. A few of the lonelier employees eyeballed the girl whenever she passed their work areas; about three men and two women, this time around. Considering that number changed daily, there was no denying the cold, hard truth.

She was beautiful, but oh-so-strange.

Rosemary Louise Demore had no issue with that, however; all of the most iconic people in the world were a little strange. Jim Morrison, Morrissey, and Dan Aykroyd were great examples. Granted, the blonde wasn't much of a musician, but Aykroyd was a big inspiration to her for his theories on UFOs and aliens. Hearing him in interviews inspired her to do a little research of her own.

Now she was the host of her own podcast during her off time. Working for this consultation office as a stockroom lackey was only to pay the ludicrous Central Florida bills. If anyone had ever told Rosemary how expensive of a city Orlando was, she never would've moved there after dropping out of college. She would've stayed in Delaware with her mom and pop.

But alas, she was far from home and willing to make a living doing what she did best; following orders while her real fight lied in her voice over a boom mic. If getting the truth out meant slaving away at a dead end job, then Rosemary would do it for all eternity. The people deserved better than those hacks who spewed bullshit over so-called "podcasts" and then went on hiatus for many years at a time. No, she would be a diligent, prolific host for her adoring fans; all one hundred and ten of them.

But for now, none of those viewers could listen to her. Rosemary was tasked with checking the break room's stock. God forbid the office drones surrounding her run out of coffee. Didn't they know that the government encouraged everyone to have crippling caffeine addictions? It was the simplest way to increase productivity, which in itself only served to make the sheeple fall in line with the well-oiled machine that was capitalism.

Capitalism led to poverty.

Poverty led to exposure.

Exposure led to death.

It was the perfect plan.

Nobody understood her logic, sadly. She tried explaining this simple premise many times to her co-workers, and they just rolled their eyes. "Shut up," they'd tell her. "I *need* my coffee to put up with this shit."

The frustration overwhelmed Rosemary sometimes. But once she made it to the break room, she stopped dead in her tracks. Sitting at the white table and sipping a cup of Joe was the one person she wished more than anything would listen to her gospel. If anyone needed to be saved from the government's deception, it was this man.

Mister Chad Singer.

CEO of the company.

Rosemary's boss.

The most perfect man in the world.

He was dark-skinned with short, black hair. Oak wood brown eyes graced his baby face. His suit jacket barely fit over his enormous chest and arms. The muscles on this guy! He looked like he'd been working out every day after work for a few years.

Mister Singer looked up at Rosemary and wiggled his nose. "Ah, hello...uh, Rhonda? Rose?"

She smiled wide. "Rosemary, sir. And it is a delight to see you this morning."

The CEO snorted, taking another sip of his coffee. "That's not news to me. I'm a treat to everyone I encounter."

She giggled nervously, straightening herself up so she didn't look like a slouching mess. "So, how are you, sir?"

She hoped he'd put down the white coffee mug. He didn't need to develop a caffeine addiction when he was so healthy and handsome. She wished he'd drop to his knees and beg her to save him. But more than anything, she secretly begged him to confess his ungodly attraction to her.

"You're so beautiful in that dress," she wished he'd say. *"Those eyes of yours drive me wild. I'd make love to you right now if we weren't stuck in this shabby office."*

But sadly, none of her wishes came true.

Chad held on to his coffee mug and scowled at the stockroom girl. "I'm anxiously waiting for you to leave me alone so I can finish my coffee in peace. Don't you have a toilet to unclog or something?"

Rosemary's smile never wavered. The sheer fact he was talking to her made her dead-end job seem less depressing. If only she could have the courage to ask him on a date. She didn't have much money on her; he'd likely have to pay for the dinner. But she'd inspire him. She'd make him laugh. She'd make him *sweat*.

But in the meantime, all she had was her fantasies.

Maybe one day a miracle would shine down upon her.

Maybe one day, Chad Singer would be hers.

2

∾

A Pleasant Surprise

Come four in the afternoon, Rosemary had clocked out at work. Nobody wished her well as she left the tall skyscraper of a building, but that was okay. Now that the drudgery of day jobs was over for the time being, now was the time to follow her true passion. But first, she'd have to make the journey through Downtown Orlando.

Working downtown had its perks, but also its fallbacks. On one hand, the city was lively and colorful on the darkest of days. Something was always going on, whether it be a protest, a parade, or simply some kind of arts and culture event. Orlando couldn't be called boring, by any stretch of the imagination.

On the other hand, *the city was lively and colorful on the darkest of days*. That meant traffic was always congested. There were lots of honking cars, swearing drivers, and potential road rage scenarios. Not to mention the sheer amount of school zones one had to cross through! And Rosemary had the misfortune of needing to cross through at least two elementary schools during her daily commute home.

So as Rosemary made her way to her 2015 modeled KIA Soul, gray as a cloudy day, she mentally prepared herself for the clogged roads of Orlando. She climbed inside her car, buckled up, and stuck the key into the ignition. Blasting at full volume was an audiobook about the forming of historical monuments.

"How exactly did the Egyptians build such majestic monuments back in the day?" Professor Franklin Burton of Maine University asked. *"They hadn't the supplies nor the resources to build the pyramids! That tells me that they didn't build them at all, for the pyramids were built by forces beyond our understanding."*

The young woman nodded in agreement and shifted the car into reverse. She backed out of her parking space, turning the car left. Then she shifted back to drive and exited the ramp, leading into the wild streets. If she could beat the red lights, she'd possibly make it home in about ten minutes.

As she drove, the strong air conditioning blew into her face, making her hair flap in the small space of the Soul. The words of Professor Burton rang in her ears like holy gospel. *"While we're on the subject of the pyramids, has anyone ever wondered what the Great Sphinx is supposed to represent? Modern day archeologists suggest that it's a nod to their gods, but I beg to differ."*

Rosemary listened closely, weaving through traffic like a needle sewing up a hole in a shirt. Plenty of cars honked at the twenty-two-year-old, and one man even flipped her the bird as she cut him off. In her hometown, she'd never think to drive so recklessly; there was never a need to. Drivers in Blades were courteous, friendly, and often didn't resort to violence when met with someone driving five miles below the speed limit.

But in the hellscape called Orlando, the need to drive like a bat out of hell was present.

"You see," Professor Franklin continued. *"The Great Sphinx is very likely an average being living in outer space. I'd wager that the monument isn't a monument at all! It's likely alive, but we need someone brave enough to chip away the stone imprisoning the creature."*

Rosemary gasped. "No way!" She then let one hand go up to each of her ears, checking to make sure her aquamarine gemstone earrings were still secure. "I never would've thought of that. That's intense!"

It occurred to the young woman that the former professor from Maine was literally a genius. Not only was he giving her material for her own show, but he was opening her eyes to things that not even she considered. The world was a crazy place, and it was impossible to assume that humans built everything. Maybe today, sure. But back in the day, when technology was horrifically primitive? Absolutely not.

Rosemary had always been an eccentric child growing up. But her eyes weren't truly open until she was ten years old. She had stayed out on the back porch one evening while her mother cooked dinner and her father was playing with the family dog. All was calm, until one brief moment that something flew over her home. It went by so fast that it couldn't have possibly been a plane, nor was it a comet or shooting star.

"Daddy?" She pointed at the dark, starry sky. "What was that that just flew over us?"

Her pops looked up, seeing nothing of interest. "Uh, probably a bird or something, honey."

The next day at school, she went to the library and did lots of reading; more than she'd ever done in her entire school career, admittedly. She eventually came to two conclusions of what the flying object was: Superman, or a UFO. Even in her youth, she knew Superman was just a comic book character. So the only logical conclusion was that it was aliens.

Such a tiny occurrence meant everything to Rosemary, and it shaped the woman she became in the year 2017. Nothing was going to change her mind, but she could change the minds of many people if they'd only listen. Big changes were coming to the world, but nobody dared heed her warnings. It was like she was another crazy conspiracy theorist that nobody paid any mind to.

"Don't listen to Rosemary. She's crazy."

"Rosemary suffers from paranoid delusions. Don't mind her."

"Schizophrenia is a tragic disorder."

It was a maddening existence, but she'd never give up. The people deserved to know what was up with the universe. This was to be Rosemary's duty and curse. And she'd commit to this job until she was gray in the hair and dying in a hospital.

Suddenly, as Rosemary was pulling onto Colonial Drive, her console rang. The name "Dad" appeared on her screen. She smirked and pressed the green button. "Hey Daddy," she greeted. "What's up?"

"Rosie," he said, voice a little low from his old age. "I heard your latest episode of your podcast."

Her smile widened. "Oh? What did you think?"

He sighed. Rosemary could practically see him shaking his head. "Jesus was abducted by *aliens*? I can't wrap my head around that one, honey."

She brushed some hair out of her face. "There's lots of evidence that says it's true, Daddy. Just do some research and you'll see."

"Rosie," he said, voice raising a little. "Your "research" isn't from credible sources. Your mother is really worried about you. It's okay to have hobbies, but you're risking making a fool out of yourself in front of millions of people."

Rosemary rolled her eyes. This happened every time he called. She hoped, just once, he'd call and praise her for her work. But no, he had to call and give her a "come to Jesus" talk.

"Tell Mom she doesn't need to worry. I'm fine."

He sighed again. "At least use a different name instead of your birth name. That way nobody can track you and harass you over your views."

Now it was Rosemary's turn to sigh. "Whatever, Daddy. I love you. Talk to you later."

She pressed the red button on the console, ending the call.

"Dammit," she muttered to herself. "Old man just doesn't get it at all," the blonde eyeballed her reflection in her rear-view mirror, blinking once. "He'll come around. They all will, one of these days."

*****

After parking in the driveway of her house, Rosemary killed the engine in her vehicle. She leaned back into her seat and sighed heavily. "Patience is key, Rosemary," she muttered to herself. "Patience is *key*."

The blonde unbuckled her seatbelt and exited the car. She approached her front door and looked down at the keyring grasped in her hand. She spotted the house key and inserted it into the lock. With one turn, the door unlocked, and Rosemary was allowed access into her home.

Rosemary Demore lived in a modest home; one bedroom, one bathroom with a tiny kitchen and a moderately sized living room. She didn't bother to decorate much of the house, as it was being rented. Rosemary had been kicked out of another home in the past because her lease wasn't renewed; something about the owner planning on demolishing the place. She knew she'd be kicked out of this house by the end of the year, so what was the point of decorating?

Upon entry, she was greeted by her little Tuxedo cat, Roswell. "*Meow,*" he greeted, rubbing up against her legs. The young woman smiled and bent down to remove her stiletto heels. Once the shoes were off, she stepped over him, catching the hint of his affectionate behavior. She walked into the kitchen and took a look at his food bowl; still plenty of chow. "Ross, your bowl is full. Calm down."

The cat simply stared up at her with big yellow eyes.

Rosemary sighed, crouching down to scratch his chin.

This seemed to please the feline.

Once the king of the household was satisfied, Rosemary headed into her garage. She would've parked her car inside it, but Florida residents scarcely used their garages for their intended purposes. Nine times out of ten, garages were used for storage. This was partially true for Rosemary; however, she also converted it into a recording studio for her podcast.

The metal reinforcement inside the garage meant radio waves couldn't penetrate her safe haven from the insane society she lived in. The last thing she needed was for the government to try controlling her mind. They were enemies of the alien overlords in outer space, anyway. If she was ever going to meet aliens, it wouldn't be under the pretense of being brainwashed by the United States government.

This was not just an intention; it was a promise.

Pushing aside a few full boxes, Rosemary made it to her desk and took a seat. The process of setting up for an episode of her podcast was fairly simple: start up the computer, set-up the mic, click into the recording software, and have at it. It normally took five to ten minutes to have everything ready for each episode. Sometimes hiccups occurred; often in the form of her computer being bogged down with perpetual slowness.

This time around, no problems arose as she readied herself for yet another episode that would be promptly edited and uploaded by night-time. She slid her headphones over her ears, pulled the mic up to her face, and clicked the record button. "This is *World Truths with Rosemary Demore*," she started with. "This is not your schoolteacher's educational program; this is where only the relevant facts of the universe are heard. Who cares about mitochondria when the universe is so much bigger than simple cells?"

She took a quick breath. "Today, I want to review a piece of literature by Professor Franklin Burton of Maine University. I was driving to my day job this morning while listening to Burton's *Lies: A Scandalous Farce*," Rosemary paused for a moment, smiling into the mic. "I'm telling you folks, this man is brilliant. There's so many theories he's concocted that I never would've thought of."

Suddenly, the loud squeaking of unchecked brakes sounded outside Rosemary's garage. She rolled her eyes. "Fuck's sake," she mouthed. But she didn't let this noise stop her from recording.

"One such theory he had was about the Great Sphinx of Egypt," the door on the loud vehicle outside slammed shut and multiple voices started shouting at each other. The words were indistinguishable, but it was loud enough for Rosemary to consider it disruptive. She had half a mind to yell at the noisy cretins.

But alas, she persisted with her recording.

"His theory is that the Great Sphinx isn't a monument at all, but a—"

A loud slam was heard outside the garage and Rosemary took off her headphones, throwing them into the computer screen. "Who the *hell* are these people?" She stood up from her desk and stomped over to the garage door. She pressed the white button and the door slowly opened.

The source of the noise seemed to be a large mover truck. It was much larger than any mover truck she'd ever seen; it looked more like a large freight vehicle than anything else. They had the back door open and two muscular men were carrying a rather nice-looking couch down the ramp. "Someone had to have done evil things to get this house," said one mover aloud.

Rosemary looked at the house next door. It was what Floridians called a "McMansion". It looked to be three floors but had a small yard with a fountain smack dab in the middle. The blonde had wondered if anyone was ever going to buy this house; it was selling on the market for about two million dollars!

"*Who won the lottery?*" Rosemary thought to herself. She looked to the driveway for an answer to her question. Sitting there was a beautiful Tesla car, year model unknown. It was obsidian black, which was an odd choice for a color in Florida. Didn't this person know how hot this state got? Having a black car was like wrapping oneself in wool and then stepping directly in the sun's core!

Stepping out of the car was someone Rosemary never expected to see this close to her home.

Chad Singer, himself.

3

Chad's Office

The next morning, Rosemary was about thirty minutes late to work. She admittedly found herself staring outside Chad's home, waiting to see if she'd see him and have a chance to say hello. Since finding out he was her new neighbor, Rosemary hadn't had the energy to do much else but stare at the McMansion. She didn't even finish the latest episode of her podcast.

What was wrong with her?

She'd always been attracted to this man, true.

But something was taking hold of her.

Whether it was sinister or benevolent, she wasn't sure.

Granted, nobody seemed to care that she was late to work. That tended to happen when one worked in a large office with hundreds of drones typing up useless data. Her tardiness would only mean something if some kind of crisis occurred without her knowing, such as running out of coffee or paper. Oh, the people would riot if that were to ever happen!

Luckily for Rosemary, no such crisis occurred. However, she did task herself with restocking the office with printer paper, as they were down to three stacks. As many trees were killed for the sake of contracts and other documents in this place, the drones would certainly need their paper. Nobody would thank her, but that was okay.

She wasn't working this job for praise, just money.

While Rosemary lifted stacks of paper up onto the central shelf, she suddenly felt someone poke her shoulder. She turned around to see Marla, who looked like she'd just seen a ghost. "Hey, uh, Rosemary?"

The blonde tilted her head. "Yeah? What's up?"

"Mister Singer wants to see you in his office," she explained. "He says it's *dire.*"

Rosemary's eyes sparkled. "*Mister Singer wants to see me?*" She smiled wide, clapping her hands. "Awesome! I'll go see him right this second!"

"I dunno," Marla murmured. "He didn't sound too enthusiastic. I think you might've messed up something."

Rosemary blew a raspberry through her lips. "*Please.* I didn't do anything wrong. Why would he chew me out?"

Marla held her hands up. "Whatever you say. I'm just the messenger."

Wasting no time, Rosemary dropped her stacks of paper and rushed to Chad's office. This was the moment of truth, she believed. He likely saw where she lived and aimed to save her from the insane Orlando rent. "*You're living in squalor, my dear,*" he'd tell her as he caressed her face.

"Pack your things and come with me. We'll live happily in my new home and I'll cook all your favorite foods."

Or, perhaps he'd be a little risky. *"As you might've noticed, I'm unmarried, dear Rosemary. Please come over and show me how to love."*

She smiled like a maniac as she made it to his office. "Stay calm, Rosie," she told herself. "This might not be anything. Don't get ahead of yourself."

She gave the door a knock.

"Come in," Chad answered.

Rosemary opened the door and was immediately floored. She'd never been inside Chad's office before, and she was glad to have had the pleasure at least once. Red velvet carpet, creamy white walls with photos of what she assumed were Chad's family and friends. He even had a bust of himself sitting next to the door.

And in the dead center of the room was Chad himself, lifting a curl bar with at least one hundred pounds attached to it. He smelled of masculinity and heat. Rosemary was once again stifled by the beauty of this man. With sweat rolling down his shirtless body, she found herself on the verge of drooling. His torso glistened under the bright light of his rhinestone ceiling fan. If she looked too much longer, she'd go blind.

"Keep it together," she told herself. "Don't treat him like a piece of meat."

Rosemary stared at him for a hot moment, fantasizing about the sinful things she'd do to this man. He had a six pack, which she imagined herself running her hands up and down. How she longed to lick the sweat off his neck like an insatiable vampire. How she'd remove his clothes and exercise with him all night long.

And she didn't even work-out on a *weekly* basis, let alone daily.

"Miss Rosalie?" Chad greeted, sitting up from his bench. "You can quit gawking like a spastic teenager."

Rosemary pushed her jaw up, not realizing her mouth had been agape this entire time. "S-Sorry sir," she said. "I just, uh. You wanted to see me?"

"Yes," he confirmed, standing up and grabbing a hand towel from off his desk. He wiped the sweat off his face, giving Rosemary another chance to stare at him without judgment. "It's come to my attention that we are now next-door neighbors."

She smiled wide. "Yes, we are! I was afraid you'd—"

"Not notice?" He answered for her, dropping his hand towel onto the floor. "Don't worry, I noticed," he sighed, shaking his head. "Kind of hard not to when you see some psycho staring at your house in the early hours of the morning."

She giggled, looking down at the floor. "You have a nice house, sir. I've always dreamt of having that house."

"Yes," he said, looking up at Rosemary. "Well, *lucky me.*"

He stepped forward, placing a hand on her shoulder. Her eyes widened. He was touching her! Physical contact with the most perfect man in the world!

"I'm gonna have to ask you to stop staring at my house," Chad dropped onto her like a ton of lead. 'If you so much as get in my yard again, I'm calling the police. Savvy?"

Rosemary's expression never changed. She was so ecstatic about him touching her that she hadn't the words to respond to him. It was like an archangel had fallen from Heaven and blessed her. Or better; an alien overlord chose her to spread the message to humankind!

"*Rory?*"

She shook her head.

"Y-Yes, sir."

Chad smirked. "Good. Now get out of my office this instant."

4

Upon Her Window

He watches soap operas in his free time.

He must be a secret romantic.

He never uses window blinds.

He wants to be seen.

He's a dirty boy.

He wants to be seen by her.

Rosemary watched Chad go about his daily after-work duties from her bedroom window. She neglected recording an episode of her podcast that evening, as there was a far more interesting show she needed to engage herself with. She needed to see Chad watch his favorite shows on TV. She longed to see him cook dinner for himself and his little chow-chow.

He was a lover of animals.

Good to know.

Every little move he made; she watched him like a hawk. When he scratched his ass, she noticed with intrigue. When he rubbed his nose with his forearm, she giggled like a little girl playing with dolls. In the end, perhaps he *was* her doll to play with. She longed to hop him up and down as she played with his beefy arms and legs.

Granted, she wanted him to hop up and down on her.

But that would come later...in more ways than one.

A part of the blonde woman felt disgusted by her behavior. What was wrong with her? Why was she obsessing over this man? She'd never had a boyfriend in her entire life. Even *she* knew this wasn't the way to get one. So why do it? Why lust after the perfect man?

Because he was the perfect man.

He was like the Heisman trophy if it were a human being. That made her wonder if he'd ever played football? The thought of him tackling other hunks on a field littered with fake grass and dirt made her heart pitter-patter. "Stop this," she whispered. "This is wrong."

But he was just so beautiful. Chad Singer was the most majestic man in the entire world. He was confident, he was successful, he was rich...what wasn't there to love about him? He was everything Rosemary wished she could be and more!

Currently, Chad was shaving in his bathroom. He was running a tiny razor across his jaw, cutting up the stubble. What Rosemary would've given to run her hands across the tiny hairs poking out of his face. What she would've given to rub her hand across his smooth face.

Soon, the dark-skinned boss man nicked himself on the chin. A thin line of blood ran down his jaw. She didn't have a very good view, but his mirror told the entire story that she needed to hear. Chad grabbed a wad of toilet paper and held it against his chin.

She wondered if he was growling.

Ooh, she loved hearing men growl.

It was so enticing; so *sexy*.

Rosemary sighed. She was a hot mess. Obsessing over this man like he was another alien sighting. She was neglecting her duty to inform the masses of the cold hard truth. He was no overlord from space, but he was second best in her eyes. Being second best in Rosemary Louise Demore's eyes was an honor in itself, really. Who *wouldn't* want to be idolized by her?

"I need to get recording," she muttered to herself. "But *hot damn*, I need to keep watching."

Chad, none the wiser, dropped the bloody toilet paper and continued to shave his face like nobody was watching him. He eventually set the razor down and removed his shirt. Rosemary swooned, finding herself drooling at the sight before her. He then unbuttoned his pants. It was a shame she couldn't see his lower half as he stripped in front of his mirror.

The CEO then turned the shower knob, water shooting down like an angry thunderstorm. He climbed into the shower and started rubbing himself all over. This man had to have known she was watching. There was no other explanation for this intentional voyeurism!

He wanted her to see him.

He wanted to tease her.

He wanted to titillate her.

And *by God* was it working.

It was settled then. Rosemary Demore had to have Chad Singer. But he seemed to want nothing to do with the blonde at work. But these actions at home? That spelled a different word for the young woman.

If he was going to play hard to get, then Rosemary clearly needed to play dirty to win Chad's heart. Should she strip in front of her window; entice him from afar? No, that wouldn't do. He may not notice, plus some random pervert may see her. She couldn't have that!

Should she make a public show of her affection at work? Perhaps she could bring him flowers, chocolates, and serenade him with her favorite long song? No, he'd turn her down because it was around others. He had to maintain a professional appearance, after all.

Maybe some classic, like a love letter that she'd slide underneath his office door? She would've considered it, but then flashbacks of her high school days bite her on the ass. The notes she'd given to the boys were the same ones who proceeded to bully her nonstop for weeks on end. They only left her alone when it wasn't fun anymore.

Then, it hit Rosemary like a freight train.

Why not kidnap Chad Singer?

If she forced him to see the real her, he'd realize he loved her all along. If he saw who she was outside of her job as a stockroom girl, he'd drop to his knees and beg her to take him. It was the perfect plan. It made the most sense out of any other possible plan.

But what if he called the police?

Easy, she'd tie him up so he *couldn't* call.

Kinksters loved being tied up, after all.

Rosemary was risking her entire life doing this. If she were caught, she'd be arrested so fast. She'd get many years in prison. She'd lose her job, maybe put on some kind of exclusive list.

Rosemary didn't care.

She needed Chad Singer's body.

She needed his soul.

She was going to make him hers.

And he was going to love every second of it.

5

༄

You Can Be Mine

"Hey, printer lady. *Printer lady.*"

Rosemary blinked rapidly, realizing she'd spaced out for the eightieth time in the span of her shift. Every single time she'd come even remotely close to Chad Singer's office, her mind would drift. Her attention would sour to those around her. The people working in this building? Nothing. The printer lacking paper? Nothing. The old coffee grounds burning in the break room?

Nothing, nothing, nothing.

None of these things were important to Rosemary Louise Demore.

She was on a mission, a mission for love.

So, when the worthless peon of an office drone barked at her at the printer, the blonde glared at him. "I'm sorry. Who are *you*?"

The middle-aged, balding man stepped back. His mouth was agape, eyes bulging out of his head. "I-uh-just wanted to print something."

Appropriately standing her ground, Rosemary dropped the stack of papers onto the counter. A loud thud made the man jump. "Well then. Load up the printer, Ken."

The man, still profoundly dumbstruck by the audacity of this woman, shook his head. "Bill. My name is *Bill*."

The young woman scowled. "Bill, Bob, Ben. I don't give a damn what your name is. You are *beneath* me," she eyeballed Chad's door again, smiling smugly. "I'm in with an important crowd. You aren't worth my time."

It was true. Rosemary was next-door neighbors with the big boss man. As far as she was concerned, they were practically married at this point. All she needed to do was make her intentions very clear to this man. He needed to know how much she yearned for him.

And surely, he'd yearn for her, too.

"Oh-Kay," Bill murmured. "You're obviously crazy. Please, just do your job and restock the printer. I have reports that are due by the end of the day."

Rosemary slammed her fists into the table. "I *said* I'm better than you! You have arms. Do it your *fucking* self!"

The man threw his arms up. "That's it. I fucking quit. I *quit*. I don't get paid enough to put up with crazy bitches." With that, Bill stormed off down the row of cubicles, eventually making it to the elevators at the end of the office. Whatever his fate was from that point on, Rosemary cared not. She meant it when she said he was beneath her.

Though, to waste time before Chad left for the day, Rosemary decided to go ahead and restock the printer anyway. She did it because she felt like it, not because some peon told her to. The only man allowed to order her around was Chad Singer, and *boy* would he do loads of ordering later when she whipped out the rosé and music.

She wagered that Chaddy-Boy was quite the kinkster.

He certainly carried himself like someone who was dominant in bed.

All the more exciting for the young woman!

Once the printer was once again full of paper, Rosemary spent the next couple of minutes obsessing over the wooden door that was between her and her beloved. It was a simple door, but it signified much to the girl. Doors, especially wooden ones, could easily be hacked to pieces. It happened all the time in horror movies, and for good reason.

If Rosemary were a mere barbarian, she'd just crush that door to bits and steal Chad Singer away from whatever insignificant task was keeping him from her. If anybody were to try stopping her, she'd chop them with her mighty ax. Nothing would stop her, if she had the upper body strength to carry out this fantasy.

Alas, she was a small woman. Opening jars was enough of a challenge, as it was! So Rosemary was going to have to go the old-fashioned way of kidnapping. Before stepping into work that morning, Rosemary had snuck inside her local pharmacy and managed to get her hands on some chloroform and some tissues.

The plan was simple.

Get Chad alone and knock him out.

Simple enough.

So when the end of her shift came, Rosemary casually clocked out like nothing was going on. She was just going to go home and record her little podcast again, right? Wrong...ish. She'd still record her show, but she'd have a special guest on air with her; whether he wanted to be there or not.

To not raise too many suspicions, Rosemary parked her KIA Soul across from Chad's black Tesla. She knew it was his, as she'd taken the time to carefully memorize his license plate. It read "T2HHRT." Quite the ironic plate, considering Rosemary's line of work.

Thankfully, Florida license plates were already easy to memorize. Just six digits was all it took to frame somebody of a crime in these parts. But it was Rosemary's hope that nobody would get in trouble for what she was going to do today. She didn't plan on hurting Chad, unless he specifically asked her to.

After about an hour of waiting in the hot Florida heat, Rosemary caught sight of Chad Singer making his way to his pretty electric car. He had taken off his suit jacket, tossing it over his shoulder as his huge chest muscles practically burst through his white button-up. Was it possible for there to be a more perfect man in the world? No, there was not. It was humanly impossible.

The woman smiled wide as she started up her engine. Coming on her radio was another talk from Professor Franklin Burton of Maine University. This time, she had stopped him in the middle of explaining the Lost City of Atlantis. "*...and why can't we find this holy city, you may ask? Simple. It's been hidden away for every manner of human being. The only ones who can access it are beyond this world.*"

Rosemary nodded as she shifted into reverse. "Spoken like a true genius," she stated as-a-matter-of-factly. "You and I are kindred spirits,

Mister Burton." Once she backed out, she began to follow Chad's Tesla to the end of the parking lot, keeping her distance so as to not give herself away too soon.

It would be a slow drive back home, but well worth it.

6

A Likable Heroine

"Don't despair, dear listeners," exclaimed the esteemed Professor Franklin Burton of Maine University. *"It's only a matter of time until higher beings decide to communicate with us mere mortal humans. We're such a fascinating species, after all! Who wouldn't want to talk to us?"*

Rosemary scowled as she listened to the radio. *"I* don't want to talk to us," she sneered. "People's heads are too empty. They don't want to look at what's right in front of them," as she said this, she followed Chad Singer from a safe distance. The young woman allowed two cars to get in front of her as she rode down Robinson Street. There was no need to spook him and make him stray any further from her love.

"Human beings just have no self-awareness at all."

Traffic began to pile up, but Rosemary didn't let that detract her from the objective at hand. If anything, it gave her more time to ease her nerves about the nefarious plan she was about to enact. Was she sick to be even thinking about kidnapping her boss?

No, of course not!

It was everyone else who was sick in the head!

Butterflies fluttered in her stomach as they inched closer toward their residences. The plan was going to be as simple as one, two, three. One, two, three, the lovely prick gets drugged and tossed into Rosemary's garage. If only she had remembered to buy roses; then the escapade would've been even more romantic!

Suddenly, flashing lights glared into her rear-view window. Glows of red and blue made her heart race. "*Shit*!" The tell-tale call of the police siren blared in her ears.

There was no denying it.

Her love begets misfortune.

"*Pull over the vehicle.*"

Rosemary contemplated her next move for a span of five seconds. Should she surrender to the law, or pursue her life's greatest treasure? "*Fuck*," Rosemary exclaimed. "What do I choose?! My record, or my love?"

Well, she thought to herself.

The answer was very clear.

And so, Rosemary floored it, speeding off away from the police. Soon enough, the sounds of a blaring siren echoed throughout the city of Orlando. She was already going to break the law today; what wasn't more crimes on top of kidnapping? After all, Rosemary was a very likable woman. Chad would see that soon enough, as soon as she could shake off the cops.

So, she floored it, making her car screech loudly. "Eat my shit," she muttered as she weaved around traffic, even passing Chad's Tesla. She knew where he was going. She'd get her hands on him one way or another.

"You know, there is significant evidence that higher life-forms have infiltrated the White House," Professor Franklin Burton explained. *"Why else would the democrats try to change the way things have always been in this country?"*

Rosemary would've nodded in agreement, but she was too busy fleeing from the iron grip of the law. Meanwhile, the cops were still screeching commands at her. *"Pull over the vehicle now! This is OPD!"*

The blonde looked up at her rear-view mirror, noticing the squad car barreling down on her. It was a mere two feet from her bumper. "Fuck," she through to herself. This plan was a disaster. Thanks to the pigs in blue, she was going to miss out on her opportunity to catch her boss when he least expected it. Dammit!

"There has to be some way outta here," she murmured. Even if she managed to shake these boys, they still had her license plate number. They had a name to attach to the vehicle. They would find her and take her away from her beloved Chad. That is unless they made the assumption that the vehicle was stolen...which was entirely possible.

...

Then Rosemary had an idea; a wicked idea, at that.

She had reached eighty miles per hour on a stretch of road lacking heavy traffic, save for a few stragglers. Once she noticed the growing number of squad cars following her, the blonde made her big move.

Rosemary stomped on her brakes and made a sharp turn left. Due to her Kia Soul being a compact vehicle and not having the wherewithal to successfully make such a turn, the car flipped over onto the street, sliding so the vehicle laid horizontally to the road.

"*Oh shit*!" Rosemary screamed as she felt her head bang against the steering wheel, deploying the airbag into her face. The windshield cracked and the driver's side window shattered, digging glass shards into the girl's arm; just what she hoped would happen. As the vehicle lay upside down, she felt cool blood slowly leak over her forehead and onto the airbag. Thankfully, the girl had enough sense to wear her seatbelt. Otherwise, she'd probably been dead.

"Sh...Shnap outta it, Rosemary," she slurred, eyesight blurring. She most certainly had a concussion from this ballsy move of hers. "I gotta...gotta get outta here." And with that, Rosemary's shaky hands grabbed onto the outside of the broken window. She pulled herself out as quickly as she could.

She crawled out onto the glassy street, wincing as shards dug into her palms. Not looking to hurt herself in vain, she stood up and made a mad dash away from the sight of the wreck. The cops, luckily, swerved away from her car and ended up wrecking themselves. One slammed into a pole, another flipped upside down and collided into her totaled car, and the third slammed headfirst into his upside-down buddy.

"Idiots," she mumbled as she escaped the scene of the crime. She giggled weakly, realizing that these cops were probably dead and wouldn't be running after her. But hey, that was life. You win some, and you lose some. It wasn't her fault the cops were inept enough to allow themselves to hurt themselves in the midst of a chase.

And so the eager beaver made the long haul home, anxiously waiting to hold her future lover in her arms.

***

Body bloodied from the rough excursion with the police, Rosemary finally made it home with a noticeable limp. She was dizzy, disoriented, and tired. Maybe she could hold off on her plan until tomorrow? Give herself some time to recover? Maybe give herself the opportunity to come up with a less devious plan to reel in Chad Singer?

No way, buster.

After all she'd been through, she would hate herself for giving up now. She needed to follow through with her plan. She needed to make Chad love her.

So she limped over to his yard, blood dripping onto his grass. Once she dragged her feet to his door, she cleared her throat. Rosemary then reached into her pocket, pulling out a white rag and a small bottle of chloroform. She doused the chemicals onto the rag.

She wasn't going to hurt him, oh no. She wasn't going to do any freaky sex type things to him while he was asleep. If she was going to make love to him, she wanted him awake to enjoy the experience.

No, sexual assault was not in the books.

She just wanted him in a state that made it easy to drag his body.

"Here goes nothing," she whispered as she pressed the finger into his doorbell button. The chime echoed both in and out of the McMansion. Within a few long moments, Chad eventually opened the door. His eyes were wide and his jaw was dropped.

"Rosa? What the fuck are you doing here? What did I say about trespassing onto my property?"

With no words and shaky hands, Rosemary grabbed him by his hair and shoved the rag against his mouth, placing her hand high enough so his nose would get a good whiff. He tried to pull away, but the woman had grabbed him by his roots. If he pulled away, he'd lose a good chunk of hair. His angry screams were muffled into the rag; his oh so beautiful screams. What pipes on this man!

Eventually, his eyes grew heavy and he dropped onto the floor.

Rosemary smiled wide as she looked down at his body.

"You're mine now."

7

Courting Mister Singer

It was funny. For a muscular man, Chad Singer looked awfully help-less as he sat on the metal chair, tied up tightly with rope Rosemary had purchased from her local hardware store. She was sure to tie him extra tight, as the blonde feared he'd use natural strength to break free. She could only imagine how sexy he'd look, breaking effortless from her dastardly clutches, flexing his muscles like a champion bodybuilder.

Jesus, she needed to get laid.

Hopefully Chad would be the one to rise to the occasion.

Rosemary looked upon the man who would soon be her mate as she wrapped a bandage around her palm. She never thought that her first real relationship would be with a hostage. She supposed every couple had their own quirky stories. How odd could they possibly be?

Her grandfather met her grandmother while she was working as a car-hop in the 1950's. Her father met her mother at a Scorpions concert in the 1980's. Chad met Rosemary as her boss until she kidnapped him in 2017. It was a much spicier love story than most, that was certain.

"I can't wait to kiss you," she murmured as winced from the sting in her hand. "I bet you taste like chocolate strawberries." She licked her lips as she eyeballed the dark piece of meat before her. "Bet you're juicy like a strawberry, too."

Once the bandage wrap snapped, she fastened the medical tape over her bloody hand. Rosemary still felt pain in her legs and hips, but that's the price to pay for getting in an overly-dramatic car accident.

Mom always did tell her that she was one for theatrics.

Dad just looked concerned, as he always did.

"I wanna tell you my life story, *Chaddy-Waddy*," she sang. "I'm sure it will excite you. It's quite a riveting tale, if I do say so myself." She paced back and forth in front of the unconscious man, humming to herself. "Where do I begin?"

Rosemary's eyes locked onto the fan on her ceiling, her expression growing manic. "When I was a little girl, I saw a UFO in the sky. It flew at supersonic speed," she smiled wide, turning to look at her captive lover. "My parents just thought I was being an imaginative little girl. But I knew better than that. I *always* know better than that!"

She threw her arms out, shouting her next couple of words. "I saw the *truth*! I *know* what's watching us! And I will let *everyone* know!" she ran over to her garage window and slapped her hands into the glass. "You hear me, world?! I *will* get through to you! You *will* say I'm important! Because I am. I'm *so* important! Don't fucking forget that."

As she huffed and heaved, she slid her hands down from the window as she turned to check if Chad had awoken. "And you will be by my side the whole way through." She sauntered over her way, swinging her hips.

"You wanna know why? Because you're *mine*. I claim you. I love and adore you, Chad Singer. And we're meant to be together."

Finally, after what seemed to be an eternity, Chad began to groan and twitch his nose. Rosemary's heart began to pound as she now hovered over him, watching her boss like a hawk. "Yes, my pet. Wakey-wakey. Let me love you, darling."

He opened his eyes, he smiled lazily at Rosemary. "Hey."

A loud squeal left her mouth. "*Hi*!"

Chad's eyes then widened, the realization finally hitting him like a two-ton diesel truck. "Where the *hell* am I? What are *you* doing here, Rosie?"

She took a quick breath, which was an attempt to not hyperventilate, an attempt in vain, of course. She had to think fast. If she told him the truth, he'd think she was crazy and try to escape. If she could fool him, then more power to her and her love. "I-I rescued you! Yes. Some crazy bitch drugged you and I killed her for you. I-I just got here to untie you!"

He cocked an eyebrow. "You...*killed* a woman for me?"

Rosemary nodded so hard that her neck popped. "Yes! I'd kill for you anytime, Chad! I lo—"

"Where's the body?"

She stopped mid-sentence, now hugging herself. "Body? What body?"

Chad sighed deeply. "You killed my captor. Where is the body? How did you kill her?"

Scratching at her arms, Rosemary giggled nervously. "I strangled her. She's in my backyard, in a hole I dug up!"

The big dark-skinned man squinted at his savior. "You killed my captor, buried her in your backyard, and came to rescue me, who just so happens to be tied up in *your* garage?"

Rosemary's eyes widened. "Uhm, uh. She broke in."

"And tied me up," Chad reiterated. "In your private residence."

She groaned, growing annoyed with the direction of the conversation. "*Yes.* I don't know what's so hard to understand about this, Chad. You live next door to me. My house is the ideal place to bring you."

"Why not my house?" Chad inquired. "I have a much bigger residence with more valuable items than anything you could *possibly* own."

She glared at him. "Hey, *fuck you.* My recording equipment is my life. I spent my life savings on this studio!"

Chad sneered at the blonde. "Answer my question. And, while you're at it, answer another glaring question. If you're rescuing me, why haven't you untied me yet?"

Rosemary growled loudly and slapped him hard in the face. "*Shut up*! Stop making this harder than it needs to be!"

He wiggled his jaw and looked up at her. "Why don't we just cut the bullshit and get down to brass tacks. *You* are the bitch who captured me. There's no dead body."

Rosemary let out a deranged giggle and raised her hand up to her face. She caressed her own cheeks. "Correction: there's a couple of dead bodies. The cops thought it was funny to try stopping me from getting to you."

Chad's eyes widened and his jaw dropped. "*What*? Are...are you insane?"

The blonde laughed suddenly, eyes growing to the size of dinner plates. "What's so insane about my love for you? Love isn't supposed to make sense, dumbass. It doesn't make it insane!"

"When you fucking *tie me up*, all manner of sanity is thrown out the window!" Chad argued.

Rosemary's eyes glowed under the garage light. "You aren't into bondage. Duly noted."

With a sexy growl, Chad began to struggle against the rope tied around his body. "Let me go, you vile woman! We aren't *ever* getting together. Do you understand me?"

The blonde giggled and shook her head. "You say that now, but you can't tell the future, Chad Singer. Love doesn't care about now, honey. It cares about later. And I *promise* you will adore me later. Perhaps by the end of the day."

He bit his bottom lip and rocked back and forth in his chair, trying to escape. "What are you going to do to me, Rosalie? Are you going to assault me? Because you're a toothpick. I doubt you'll get too far."

Rosemary stood up on her tiptoes and rocked back and forth on her heels. "Baby, I would've done that already if I was gonna. I want our lovemaking to be magical for both of us."

Chad held his breath, filling his cheeks for a moment before exhaling.

"So you recognize that this is wrong and you're *still* going through with it?" He jerked around in his chair for another moment before sharing more thoughts. "Well, at least you have a *little bit* of a conscience," the boss man sighed. "Not much of one, however."

The blonde continued to rock on her heels, mulling over his words. Did he really think so lowly of her? How could he say she lacked a conscience? She wasn't trying to kill him or anything! What was his problem?

"I'm not so bad, you know," she argued. "I have a cat. I show compassion to animals. I care about the betterment of humanity! You don't know me, Chad."

"So *why* would you believe I'd fall in love with you?" he asked, raising his voice. "I know nothing about you! Having a cat means *jack shit* to me. And how am I supposed to believe you're a good person when you've got me trapped in your fucking garage?"

Rosemary scoffed. "I know the truth about the universe! I know we aren't alone; we never were!"

With a groan, her boss jerked around in his rope prison. "*Please.* Spare me your crazy alien conspiracy theories."

The blonde gasped, now tugging at her hair. "It's *not* a conspiracy theory, Chad! There's *proof* that what I'm saying is straight facts! Just look it up!"

"How am I going to look up *anything* right now?" he snapped. "My arms are useless. Besides, how am I supposed to believe anything you say when you have no shred of evidence on hand?"

Biting her inner cheek, Rosemary began to feel desperate. How dare he question her? She just *knew* she was right, dammit! Nobody had ever given her this much pushback. She didn't like the way she felt and he would be so sorry he ever questioned her.

The blonde stormed over to her desk and snatched her podcast notes from off the surface. "I have *so* much evidence, Chad Singer. Look at the Great Sphinx. The Eiffel Tower. *The White House*! We didn't build those! We haven't the intellectual inclination to build such majesties! Why don't you understand me?"

Chad rolled his eyes, letting out another sigh. "Yes we did, you fucking tart. Architects banded together in both modern *and* ancient times and designed those wondrous structures. Think before you speak, Rhonda."

Steam metaphorically spewed out of Rosemary's ears. How *dare* he? How could he just sit there and doubt the hard facts she had presented him with? It was *right there*. The evidence was all around them! Why couldn't he see that? Was he just too stupid to see the truth?

Perhaps she was wrong about Chad Singer.

Maybe they weren't meant to be.

She couldn't love a man who was too stupid to keep up with her.

"My name is *Rosemary!*" the blonde screamed, slapping the bull-headed man in the face again. The sheer amount of force she put into her attack was strong enough to knock his chair over, taking him with it. He hit his head against the hard floor, yelping in pain. But she couldn't have cared less. Maybe the blow to his head would get the juices in his brain flowing!

"I will prove to you I'm not insane, you fucking asshole!"

And just like that, Rosemary stormed off and slammed the door leading to her kitchen behind her. The sound of her footsteps echoed throughout the house as she made her way to her carpeted bedroom. She yanked the doorknob and entered the room, slamming the door behind her. The blonde flopped onto her bed and instantly started crying; ugly crying, at that.

"*Why?*" she moaned. "W-Why can't he j-just *get it*?" In her violent meltdown, she began slapping the back of head. "Stupid! You're so stupid, Rosemary! Stupid, stupid, *stupid*!"

As she sobbed into her pillow, she soon felt an entity push its weight beside her on the bed. When the fuzzy face brushed against her side, she knew it was Roswell coming to check up on her. He was such a good boy, comforting his mother like that. Rosemary truly didn't deserve such a beautiful soul.

The blonde sniffled and reached to pet Roswell's warm fur coat. "T-Thank you, Ross." The amount of patience this cat was showing her was inspiring. Even at her ugliest, he found beauty in her very existence. He loved her regardless.

Suddenly, Rosemary had an epiphany.

"Of course!" she exclaimed, her mood taking a complete one-eighty. "I need to show Chad the same level of patience! He's just confused, is all. Yeah! I'll help ease him into the truth!"

Rosemary rose up and leaned into Roswell, giving him a kiss on the top of his head.

"Thank you, buddy. What would I do without you?"

The cat meowed in response.

8

The Truth Behind Everything

Like a musician preparing for a big performance in front of hundreds of adoring fans, Rosemary was preparing for a huge audience of thousands. While it was usually an easy process for the blonde beauty, something was different about this particular set-up. Instead of simply setting up the computer, she had to dust off her monitor, so it looked presentable to her lovely guest of honor. A smidge of rust kissed the boom mic, which required Rosemary's immediate attention. She couldn't have Chad see a low-quality piece of equipment!

Her voice needed to sound as crisp as bacon.

Her flow needed to be like water.

She needed this to be perfect.

Yes, a fair amount of preparation was necessary for recording a single episode of such a monumentally important podcast. Unlike the tuning of a musician's guitar, Rosemary had to actually do the work herself. But like a musician, she had to test the volume controls and make sure the boom mic wasn't sending feedback through the speakers. It would've been embarrassing to upload an episode for her audience, only to realize that she sounded like she was talking inside a microwave as it popped popcorn!

Indeed, musicians perform for hundreds, but the blonde trailblazer was performing for thousands, maybe even millions. Def Leppard might've been performing, but she was Led Zeppelin...she thought. Was Led Zeppelin the better band?

Musical oblivion aside, the blonde would prove to Mister Chad Singer that she was the hottest podcaster to ever grace the internet. He'd go from being a skeptic to being the most devout follower of the truth. He'd be a groupie evolved from a hater. This was an outcome that was *going to happen*, no question about it.

She could almost taste his perfect lips.

As Rosemary adjusted her settings, Chad remained tied to his wooden chair. He smelled of sweat, as he'd been trapped for quite a while. He'd surely need to use the restroom before long, but Rosemary couldn't allow it. What if he tried to escape?

He'd call the cops on her.

He'd get the court involved.

He'd move far away.

Worst of all, he'd die a blissfully ignorant man!

He'd be on the wrong side of humanity's fate!

By not being aware of the grand scheme, he'll be doomed to face certain extermination at the hands of vengeful sheeple who chose to ignore the will of the overlords of space. The blonde refused to let that happen. If that meant Chad having an accident in her vicinity, then it was worth it; personal hygiene be damned! So, the blonde paid no mind to the moans and groans stemming from her boss. She'd tend to his needs later.

For that moment, she had a show to do. "Testing," she said over the boom mic, listening for any unwanted feedback. When she heard a crackle follow her voice, she adjusted the volume settings on her computer. "Testing. One, two. Testing." When nothing responded to her words, she moved her focus onto the volume control. No feedback was great, but would her audience be able to hear her?

"One, two, three. Testing one, two, three," her voice played back softly through the speaker, the meter on the little digital box spiking up. Rosemary turned to face Chad and gave him a thumbs up. "We're all set." The dark-skinned man didn't respond, preferring to rest with his eyes closed.

Not looking to waste another moment, Rosemary took her seat. "Okay," she breathed, grabbing her headphones and sliding them over her ears. She clicked a few buttons on her computer, hovering her finger over the mouse for the final click until showtime. She closed her eyes and took a deep breath.

This was it.

Her moment to impress Chad Singer.

Nerves engulfed her as she sat there, shaking.

With a deep breath, she opened her eyes.

"Three, two, one..."

The blonde clicked the record button and opened her eyes. "Hello everyone! Welcome back for another *thrilling* episode of *World Truths With Rosemary Demore*. I'm your host, Rosemary Demore." The blonde looked over at her future lover. "I'm honored to bring a very special guest on today's show, ladies and gentlemen. A man with the most beautiful oak brown eyes I've ever seen," she smiled wide as the words flowed through her lips like the pouring of fine wine. "He has my heart, mind, body, and soul. He is my lover; Mister Chad Singer."

Much to the blonde's dismay, the boss man groaned loudly. "Somebody! *Anybody*! Is this live?! Someone get me out of here! This psycho has kidnapped me!"

Widening her eyes, Rosemary quickly removed her headphones and rushed over to the captured man. "That's enough out of you," she growled, grabbing a roll of tape from out her back pocket. She pulled a swath out and ripped it, slapping it over Chad's mouth. The blonde listened for a moment as his muffled voice collided into the adhesive.

"Much better," she murmured with a sigh. So much for impressing the man of her dreams. He was more focused on escaping; the nerve of him! She was offering him VIP access to her show and *that* was how he repaid her?

"*Great,*" she groaned. "Now what?"

For starters, she'd have to cut the recording and wipe the drive clean of the shitshow that had just been captured on audio. She didn't need hackers bringing the recording to light and getting her incarcerated. She could've just given up and accepted that Chad wasn't interested in her. Of course, any average Sally would've done that.

But Rosemary wasn't an average Sally.

She was a fighter.

She wasn't going to give up because of a few hiccups.

"I guess I need to start this show over, then," she thought out loud. Although, she supposed she could just edit the already recorded work to erase the undeserved outtake. But nah, that would've been too much work. Rosemary wanted to spend as much time as possible with Chad; regardless if he wanted her company or not. She simply couldn't let something as benign as a recording snafu get in the way of love.

So, the show would go on...as a take two.

Rosemary stepped back over to her desk and clicked the button to end the recording. "Let's try this again." she muttered, annoyed. She slipped the headphones over her head and took her seat back in her spinning desk chair. The muffled cries of her lover bounced off the walls, making Rosemary a smidge nervous.

He was being too loud.

She couldn't afford to be done in by his inability to shut up. What if an investigation was called? FBI agents would find her countless UFO and alien notes and they'd execute her on the spot. "She knows too much," they'd exclaim. "*Fire*!"

Honestly, falling in love was already a minefield even without police intervention!

"*Aha*," Rosemary gasped as an idea popped up into her head. She clicked an icon which displayed an eighth note. The program opened, showing a music player. She clicked the first song she saw, which was a soft R&B tune.

Rosemary growled. "Too quiet," she murmured. "I can still hear him.

If *I* can hear him, so can they." So the blonde proceeded to scroll through her music library.

Ballads.

R&B.

Classical.

Bubblegum pop.

None of these genres were enough to quiet down the antsy man behind her. The primary problem with Rosemary's taste in music was that it was too gentle, too soft. She needed something with more oomph. She needed to be daring if she was going to get through her podcast peacefully. Curse her dainty, feminine eardrums!

"Crap, crap, crap," she murmured as she feverishly scrolled down her playlist. Growing more and more desperate, she began to break into a sweat as nothing was leaping up to bite her on the teet. With another growl, she grabbed her hair on the left side of her head and tugged.

It was becoming evident that she'd have to fork over a couple bucks to buy some heavy rock songs from the online music store. "*Ugh*," she groaned. "I was hoping not to spend any money today. That's why I have a man here!"

The man himself, Chad Singer, continued to shout into his tape gag, jerking around as he tried to free himself. Losing her patience, Rosemary slammed her hands onto the surface of her desk. "Shut up! Just *shut up*!"

Alas, Chad's cries only grew louder. The blonde jumped up from her chair and stormed over to her would-be lover, unplugging her head-phones in the process. She grabbed his shoulders and pushed him and the chair onto the floor. "Be quiet," she ordered as Chad's skull hit the ground, knocking him out cold.

Rosemary's eyes widened, her hand covering her agape mouth. "*Chad*!" She crouched down and gave his body a good shake. "Please don't be dead. *Please* don't be dead!"

Luckily for her, he was still breathing. She sighed in relief, standing up with no more worries in the world. "I can have him listen to the audio later," she decided, rubbing her palms together. Though, to play it safe, she knew she needed to play some heavy music to drown out any pained moans that stem from the handsome devil.

So, the blonde returned to her desk and plugged her headphones into the outlet on her computer. She then sat down and hovered her hand over the mouse. She clicked on the link for the online music store, which loaded instantly. "Alrighty then," she thought out loud. "What screams loud enough to shut up a grown ass man?"

She clicked around, browsing the marketplace for anything tagged *rock* and *heavy*. It didn't take long for her to find a suitable choice. "Hmm," she hummed. "*Welcome to the Jungle* sounds like it rocks hard. It's by a band called *Guns N' Roses*, so it must be heavy, right?" Rosemary pressed the *preview* button and was instantly blown away by the loud guitar intro.

She'd accidentally raised the volume, apparently.

Must've been when she had to shut Chad's whiny mouth up.

"*Perfect!*" she cried over the music. Rosemary dragged her cursor over to the *purchase song* button. Within a few clicks, the song was in her library, and she was short a dollar fifty. It was all chump change to her, considering the cause.

She wanted to hear Chad's sexy moans.

But not right now.

Not when she had a show to do.

Rosemary cleared her throat and opened a new file, overwriting the useless audio. Rapidly clicking buttons, her music was playing and the recording was live. "Thank you for joining me on another edition of *World Truths With Rosemary Demore*. I'm your host, Rosemary Demore," she sighed quickly. "Today is a special episode of W.T.W.R.D. Why's that, ladies and gentlemen?"

She glanced over at Chad, who was still unconscious. "Because..." she continued with a smile. "...today we're going to lay out everything we know about the grand scheme. Yes, we're going to stick it to those skeptics out there. We're going to have a textbook review for the sake of educating the dumb!" Rosemary turned back around to look at her reflection shining off her computer screen.

"So, let's start from the beginning, shall we?" She took a deep breath before spewing what most would crudely refer to as "word salad". The blonde started with the Big Bang, which was actually caused by a craft collision in the solar system. See, alien civilization predated even humankind. How else would the non-humanoid creatures appear on Earth? That wasn't the work of a God!

The world was crafted by the debris of the gas cloud of a ship operated by Yahweh, who was a tall white female alien with solid black eyes. The other gas cloud was a ship operated by none other than Satan, who was a black alien with white eyes. His identity would later be changed to "Lucifer" and he'd be a fallen angel from the heavens who went bad.

This was a blasphemous claim.

Satan wasn't some evil entity.

He was a kind, gentle father who loved Yahweh very much.

The collision was entirely intentional. The loving couple knew that the velocity of their two ships would be enough to terraform an entire planet should the ships collide. "And so that's why there's so much gasses in our atmosphere," Rosemary explained. " It's a remnant of our very creation! Even life, such as birds and reptiles, are crafted from gas. Why else do you think we fart? It's to release pent up gas!"

From there, the eccentric blonde explained that the gasses released from the alien parents then formed the dinosaurs, who were actually as big as the movies made them out to be. "All this talk of them being bird-like are lies," Rosemary said. "Paleontologists are just scared of what the world would do if they knew just how mighty the dinosaurs truly were!"

The destruction of the dinosaurs was indeed caused by a meteor. Unlike humans, dinosaurs couldn't fart. The ability to release gas wasn't built into their anatomy. "The dinosaurs were flawed, it's true," Rosemary concurred. "Yahweh knew that the gasses built up in the reptiles would be strong enough to create the first human. So she sacrificed the dinosaurs so the pent-up glasses would encircle the atmosphere and create man."

It was truly riveting stuff, Rosemary thought. Who wouldn't want to be in on the truth behind the universe? "The cro-magnons of yesteryear were like babies; helpless and pure. Mother and father showed them how to build the wheel and form fire using sticks." With another quick breath, Rosemary wiped sweat off her forehead. All this teaching was giving her mind quite the work-out.

Alas, she ventured on without missing a beat. She presented her facts without delving too far deep into the evidence side of research. All this explaining was already hard enough without having to whip out the statistics and scientific mumbo-jumbo! She wanted to educate, not bore.

Eventually, Rosemary arrived at her favorite talking point, Ancient Egypt. "Did you guys know that the pharaohs weren't actually inbred? No sir! Their abnormalities cannot scientifically be explained by bad genetics, folks. The *only* explanation for this is that they were the first children of Yahweh and Satan. Venus is typically considered the romance planet because mother and father conceived their children there."

She slapped her hands onto her desk. "You wanna what else, everyone?! Venus is *hot*. The children brought the heat to Earth, and it formed multiple deserts across the planet, including Egypt! The pharaohs needed the heat, or their skin would freeze!"

The blonde's smile grew wide, her smile showing plenty of teeth. "Isn't that cool, guys?! And wait until I tell you about the pyramids and the Great Sphinx!" Rosemary took another breath. The song ended, causing Rosemary to have a short-lived panic attack. *Crap*, she thought to herself.

A lapse in judgment blocked her from approaching this situation from a methodical position. She only downloaded one song when, logically, she should've gotten ten or more to span the length of her recording. Now her recording was going to sound repetitive. But she dared not start over yet again; nor after spending so much time and breath explaining obvious facts behind life and the universe to her invisible audience.

So, at the risk of being monotonous, she decided to drag the slider back so the song would play again. She couldn't risk Chad waking up and calling for help. "So," she started, swatting hair out of her face. "The pyramids were *not* built by mere humans. How could they have been?

Technology didn't exist back then; the overlords didn't think we were ready. And you know what? They were right! Look at how badly we've fucked the planet with high grade technology!"

She glared into her reflection, feeling the anger course through her like an electrical current. "Pollution is rampant, homelessness is at an all-time high, and liberals still think they can win elections! We need to be stopped, ladies and gentlemen. It's for our own good!"

She took a second to wipe more sweat off her face. She always got so heated when talking about problems in the country. That made her a good person, she decided. Only good people care about the well-being of their homeland. Chad was wrong about her; he'd see soon.

"But I'm getting sidetracked, folks. Where was I, again?"

Suddenly, Chad let out a pained moan. He tried to speak, but his words were muffled by the tape.

Swallowing hard, Rosemary quietly turned the volume up on her computer. "S-So, back onto Ancient Egypt..." she looked back at Chad, who's eyes were fluttering as he came to. The blonde's eyes widened. "Uhm, uh, heh, so h-humans did not build a damn thing back then, guys. We were too primitive!"

Chad began to yell through his gag. Tears began to seep from Rosemary's eyes as she grew more desperate. She needed to finish this show. She needed audio evidence that she knew her shit. But she didn't want it to be peppered with cries from her beloved!

"N-*No*! O-Our alien overlords built everything! We d-did right by the pharaohs until that bastard *Moses* came around!" Rosemary gasped as panic began to encompass her. "His v-voodoo m-magic caused the p-plagues of—"

Chad's cries evolved into screams. Even the power of *Guns N' Roses* wasn't drowning out the sound. Rosemary was certain that the audience would be able to hear it over the boom mic. Rosemary had no choice but to rush over and knock Chad out again.

"Excuse me, folks!"

She removed her headphones and hopped up from her chair. "Do you mind?! I'm trying to record here!"

Chad glared at her, muttering something that sounded vaguely like profanity. They'd have to address that in couples therapy, surely. And the physical abuse, while entirely justified, was likely hurting Chad's feelings. An apology was necessary, she decided.

"Fuck it," she murmured. "I'll edit this out later," she crouched down and reached for Chad's face. "I'm sorry, honey." The blonde gave his cheek a quick caress before yanking the tape off his mouth. The boss man howled in pain.

"You could've killed me, you *bitch*. I'm sure I've got a concussion."

Rosemary glared at him. "I do too, you know. I hurt myself trying to get to you!"

Chad squinted. "Whose fault is that? If you wanted to tell me all these fascinating facts, you could've just told me without the theatrics!"

"Well, how was I supposed know—" the blonde's jaw dropped. "Wait. You...you actually believe everything I'm saying?!"

"Yes," he groaned. "I'm curious as to where the story of Moses is going."

Rosemary smiled wickedly. "I'm so glad you asked! After Moses caused the plagues of Egypt, Yahweh fired lightning at him. He was vaporized instantly!"

Chad blinked slowly. "So...Moses was killed by a..."

"Forty-watt laser beam from the sky, yes," Rosemary confirmed with a triumphant nod. "Let's not even ponder what happened to Jesus," she commented with a devilish giggle.

The dark-skinned love boat stared at her with anticipation. "Was he an alien, too?"

Rosemary blew a raspberry. "Of course not! But he was abducted by Yahweh. He's still alive today! He's working on calibrations for the mothership's computer!" Another giggle erupted from the excitable blonde. "By this point, you're probably thinking Satan is a deadbeat dad, right?"

Chad stared blankly at the woman. "I don't even—"

"Thank you for asking!" Rosemary exclaimed. "He sent his youngest son, Glorgnog, to Roswell, New Mexico. Well, one thing led to another, and we founded Area 51!"

Chad let out a nervous chuckle. "I guess you've got everything figured out, huh?"

The blonde scratched the back of her head. "I have. It's all out there, if you take the time to read."

And then, for the first time since Rosemary had taken him into her custody, the boss man smiled. The blonde's own smile widened. Seeing him happy unearthed some kind of lovely monster within her. After years of unrequited love from schoolboys, Rosemary felt herself tear up again, this time for happy feelings.

"You've really opened my eyes, Rosemary Demore."

The blonde let out an abrupt squeal. He remembered her name! "Really?"

Chad nodded. "Of course. It all makes sense now. Why don't you let me treat you to dinner? I make a *mean* beef wellington."

Rosemary gasped and nodded hard. "I'd love that! Here, let me free you!" Wasting no time, Rosemary pulled the end of the rope from out of its tight loops. Within a minute, Chad Singer was released. Now having full use of his hands, he reached up to caress her cheek.

He leaned in and kissed her.

9

⌣

A Moment To Die For

Rosemary's eyes stayed glued onto the man kissing her. It was truly a dream come true. For once, a guy was kissing her because he liked her! Take *that*, Derek Flannigan!

Back in high school, Rosemary had eyes for the class president. Derek was seemingly perfect. Freckles were sprinkled onto his cheeks and his chestnut brown hair seemingly changed color under a bright light. One day, he wrote her note and stuck it into her locker.

"Rosemary, meet me in the hallway outside U.S. History after the fourth period."

Excited, the blonde followed his directions and waited outside the classroom. Before she knew it, he snuck up behind her and bent her down like in a romance movie. He kissed her deeply, making her swoon. As he broke the kiss, the horrible sound of laughter erupted behind the class president.

There stood Derek's nameless buddies, who cackled like geese at their buddy kissing the "weird" girl. Worst of all, Derek dropped her onto the floor and turned to face his friends. *"You guys owe me a hundred bucks!"*

Realization hit Rosemary harder than the tiled floor did. Derek was *dared* to kiss her. He didn't actually like her. In fact, he found her foul. He found her to be imperfect and disgusting. It didn't matter that her breasts were bigger than any other girl's in her class.

She still wasn't enough for him.

But Chad Singer was a different animal altogether. He actually wanted to kiss her...and for *free*, too! It might've not been as impressive as the kiss with Derek Flannigan, but it was much more soulful. The sensation of his lips on hers was exhilarating, sending shivers down her spine.

When Chad finally pulled away, Rosemary whined and greedily pulled him back in for more. Her tongue swiped his bottom lip, the glossy texture proving to be satisfying to the touch. He was wearing lip balm. It tasted like honeycomb. Perhaps a small part of him knew he was going to hook up with her? Why else would he wear flavored lip balm?

Chapped lips weren't an explanation, as he was the perfect man.

Chad's mouth couldn't possibly know the misfortune of being dry.

Rosemary supposed the reason didn't matter; all that mattered was that they were making out and there was a very good chance Chaddy boy would get quite the dick flattening later. The blonde broke the kiss and smiled at the boss man. Not being subtle at all about her intentions, she rubbed her fingers over her cotton blue blouse, eventually grabbing handfuls of her breasts and pressing them together for her lover. Chad took the hint well, as he reached his hand over to her chest and caressed the top of her left breast.

Rosemary closed her eyes, moaning softly to his touch. Her heart was beating out of her chest and butterflies fluttered in the pit of her gut. Her eyes opened, hands dropped, and smile widened as she climbed on top of Chad, straddling him. She looked down at him and caressed his clean shaven jawline.

"I'm a lucky man," the boss man murmured. "Having such a beautiful lady on top of me."

Rosemary giggled, giving into the urge to bend down and plant another kiss on her lover's lips. To repay her licking him, he gave her bottom lip a gentle nibble. The blonde moaned to the sensation of his teeth bearing down on her. She was half-tempted to punch herself in the face just to see if she was dreaming.

She broke the kiss and straightened her torso back, so she was looking down at him. The blonde looked lovingly into his eyes. "I've been waiting for this moment all of my life."

Chad looked up at her and grinned. "For me?"

"For you," Rosemary purred. "For someone to see past the so-called *beauty and madness* that people say I possess."

Chad swallowed an incoming breath. "Why would anyone think you're *crazy*? You kidnapped me for a logical reason!"

"I *know*, right?!" Rosemary concurred. "How else were you going to learn the truth?!"

The dark-skinned man let out a nervous chuckle. "Well...you *do* have beauty, though."

Rosemary raised her hand up to her face and gently bit the fingernail attached to her index finger. "You really think so?"

Chad didn't respond, instead choosing to run his hands up and down her love handles. They slid over her sides with ease, making the blonde quiver. "*That feels good*," she moaned.

The boss man grinned wickedly. "Wait until you feel *this*." He bucked his hips, rubbing his clothed erection into the slit between her legs.

Rosemary gasped. "Oh, *Chad*!"

Chad bucked again.

The blonde moaned loudly as her trembling hands reached for the bottom of his tank top and hiked the shirt up to his pectoral muscles. She took a moment to admire the sight before her. His six-pack abs glistened with sweat. Rosemary just wanted to bend down and lick the moisture off his chest.

And so she did.

Her tongue gently scraped the creases in his abdominal muscles. Chad looked down at her, perplexed. "You have me under your spell and you focus on my *stomach*?"

The eccentric blonde giggled, retracting her tongue back into her mouth. "I can't help it. You're *very* sexy, Chad Singer."

The man let out a quick chuckle. "Well, uh, how does it taste?"

Rosemary's eye twitched. "Salty and erotic."

Chad's head tilted to the side; expression turned quizzical. "What does *erotic taste* entail?"

The blonde looked up, thinking. "Hmm. You know, I can't describe it. Just that it turns me on."

The boss man stared at her for a moment before shrugging. "Okay then." Without wasting another moment, Chad tugged at her blouse and pulled it over her head. He tossed it aside to admire the red bra with black trim that covered her d-cup breasts.

He whistled. "*Damn*, girl! You're packing some serious heat!"

Rosemary felt her face turn hot. "From what I'm feeling down under, so are you," she giggled. "I never knew my first time would be with a black man!"

The return of the perplexed expression on his face startled the blonde. "What's *that* supposed to mean?"

Her eyes widened. Oh shit, did she say something racist? She was only speaking her mind! She'd be lying if she said she'd fucked many black men before him! Her virgin flesh didn't care about skin color, dammit!

"I-I didn't mean anything by it! It's my first time with *anyone*! Your race means nothing to me, Chad!"

After a moment, his expression softened up. "Okay," he conceded. "It's all good. Now, why don't you put your mouth to better use than talking?"

Now it was the blonde's turn to have a quizzical look on her face. "You mean more kissing?" She leaned down and planted a kiss onto the lips of her boss. Once she pulled away, Chad chuckled.

"I mean, that works too." His left hand reached up to grab onto Rosemary's left breast again. She smiled, humming quietly.

"Don't be afraid to touch the other one."

The big man smiled. "You read my mind, baby." His right hand shot up and grabbed her other breast. With her gasping at his touch, he gave her a gentle squeeze.

"You like that?" he asked.

Rosemary nodded enthusiastically. "You're just as good at this as I imagined!"

Chad smirked. "Is that so?"

"*Yes,*" she moaned. "You're making me so *excited*!"

A cocky grin spread across his face. "I confess. I find myself enthralled with women such as yourself. A woman who dares challenge the false truths we're all led to believe."

Rosemary grinded into his hard bulge. "*Now* who's talking too much?"

Chad chuckled darkly. "Sorry. I'm just amazed by how much I didn't know."

The blonde giggled. "What can I say? I'm too smart for my own good!"

Suddenly, Chad's smile vanished, and he let go of her breasts. "Yes. I agree." Without warning, he wrapped his hands around her neck and gave it a tight squeeze.

Wide-eyed and horrified, Rosemary gasped. "Chad?! Y-You're *choking* me!"

In a turn of events that Rosemary would've never guessed would happen, Chad's eyes soon turned from their original brown to obsidian black.

"You know too much, Rosemary Louise Demore."

10

∽

Lover's Quarrel

Quickly realizing that her life was in danger, Rosemary screamed as she tried to pry the monster's hands off her neck. "*Let go of me!*"

Chad tightened his grip as he glared angrily into her eyes. "It's no use," he murmured. "You're going to die here."

The blonde gasped and wheeled, trying to cling onto any small pocket of oxygen she could muster up. Her vision began to fade as her life began to drift away. "S-Stop this!"

It was then that the lightbulb in Rosemary's head lit up.

She had a saving grace after all!

Letting go of his hands, the eccentric blonde mashed her own hands down onto his clothed manhood. She placed all of her body weight down on it, crushing his balls. Like clockwork, Chad howled in pain as the woman attacked his pelvis and crotch. The monster let go of her during his fit of agony.

Rosemary stood up quickly and backed away from Chad. Her head felt light as she tried and failed to catch her breath. Taking advantage of the man's agonized state, the blonde grabbed the rope from off the ground. "S-Stay back," she warned, arming herself. "I'll lasso you into oblivion!"

Not heeding her warning, Chad stood up and took his fighting stance. He bent his knees and held up his fists. "You've foiled our plans," he explained. "The universe needs you to go away forever."

Rosemary huffed and heaved, trying to process what this beast was trying to say. "You're *lying*," she whimpered. "You're some kind of *demon*. I won't listen to a word you say!"

Chad took a step toward her, baring his teeth. "I *can't* let you live!" he began to charge at her, making her scream.

"*You asked for it, asshole*!" Without missing a beat, Rosemary twirled the rope and launched the hoop at the monster. It successfully trapped him within the coils, lassoing him to the ground.

"*Ack*!" he yelped as the blonde hurried toward him. As Chad jerked around, Rosemary proceeded to hogtie him like he was a ravenous boar.

"Stay down, dirtbag!"

The demon groaned and moaned as Rosemary pulled a lighter from her left pocket and a pack of cigarettes from her right. Where these came from, only the overlords of space knew. Rosemary didn't even smoke! But, like a cowgirl in the old west, she lit up a smoke and shoved the stick in-between her lips.

The blonde took a quick puff and pulled the cigarette from her mouth, exhaling smoke in Chad's direction. "This planet ain't big enough for the two of us," she drawled, calm now that she knew she could overpower the demon.

Rosemary wondered if all of this was some horrible dream. Outrunning the police, wrecking her car, kidnapping Chad, hooking up with him, and now the new drama; was reality even a factor at that point? Did she just have an overactive imagination? What was even happening?

Unfortunately for the eccentric blonde, Chad was too strong for the rope. Unleashing his true power, he broke free from the lasso. Rosemary's jaw dropped, allowing the lit cigarette to fall to the floor. "How?! You weren't able to break free earlier!"

Chad cocked an eyebrow. "I thought you were just some crazy conspiracy theorist. I didn't realize just how much of a threat you really are," he glared at the woman. "*Now I know.*" He lunged at her, grabbing her by her shoulders.

Looking to fight back, Rosemary pushed him away and hunched down. "It's go time," she announced confidently. Now it was her turn to launch herself at him, tackling him to the ground. In his attempt to regain control of the battle, he rolled over so he was on top of her, reaching for her neck again.

Not one to be defeated, Rosemary rolled over both bodies again, so she was now above Chad. She locked her ankles against his sides, holding him down. His eyes widened. "What *is* this?!"

Rosemary smirked. "Jiu-jitsu, motherfucker."

Chad's expression turned into a mean stare as he grabbed the back of her shirt and tugged. Using his superior upper body strength, he stood up with the small woman's legs wrapped around his waist. Rosemary grabbed handfuls of his tank-top, pulling him back down to the ground. The monster pressed his knee into her stomach as she tugged at him.

Unlucky for him, that was exactly what Rosemary wanted him to do. Still holding onto his shirt, she pulled him over her head, slamming him on the ground behind her. The blonde quickly turned around and took his ankles, hiking them up so his legs were off the ground.

Chad grabbed onto her arm and pulled her down with him. Rosemary felt triumphant; he was starting to sweat. She knew then that she had him beat. She had truly regained control of the fight.

Unfortunately for the eccentric blonde, Chad Singer didn't play fair. He gurgled for a short moment and fired a ball of mucus and saliva from his mouth. The loogie hit the woman square on the nose, causing her to instantly let go of the demon. "*Ew*," she whined. "Ew, ew, *ew*!"

The monster stood back up. "No matter what fancy tricks you have up your sleeve, I'll persevere each and every time. I will succumb to *none* of your tactics."

The blonde frantically wiped the gunk off her face. "*So gross!*" She gagged for a moment before staring at her opponent with an icy glare. "You think you're going to win? You *really* think that?"

Chad smirked. "Of course, my dear. I'm leagues stronger than you." Popping a crick in her neck, Rosemary backed away from the freak and headed to her desk. She then bent down and fished for something under her desk.
Chad cackled. "Whatever toy you're looking for, it won't kill me."

"*Yes it will*," the blonde said in a sing-song voice.

The demon crossed his arms. "How can you possibly think you can win this fight?" Before he knew it, Rosemary pulled out a large object and stood up. She turned to face him. His jaw dropped.

She was carrying a M16 rifle with a M203 grenade launcher attachment at the barrel; single shot, commonly used in the Vietnam War. How could someone so delicate carry one of *those* beasts? The blonde shoved a grenade into the launcher and cocked the rifle. A twinkle of light sparkled in her eye.

"Because I'm the main character of this story, bitch."

Chad's black eyes widened. "You wouldn't dare! In your own home?!"

Rosemary smiled wickedly and fired the grenade at her nemesis. The blast exploded him and half of the garage. The recoil sent the blonde flying back, causing her to hit her already concussed head.

Dizziness overcame her and she passed out.

11

᭜

The Grand Scheme

"He that has eyes to see and ears to hear may convince himself that no mortal can keep a secret. If his lips are silent, he chatters with his fingertips; betrayal oozes out of him at every pore."

Sigmund Freud said that once upon a time. Rosemary always interpreted it to mean that one who stays silent when a truth must be uttered is betraying himself and everyone around him; family, friends, lovers, pets, trees planted outside his home...everyone and everything. The blonde took such a lesson to heart. She may have told lies in the past, but she never stayed quiet when a secret needed to be revealed. Sigmund Freud was quite the genius, she believed, even if he did endorse children's sexual attraction to their parents.

Yes, Rosemary spoke truths through her podcast. She has followers singing to the overlords of space and time. But was it all for naught? Was she truly a liar the whole time? Was she deceiving the masses?

That was her biggest fear upon waking up.

Initially, she felt a sense of relief knowing that everything that

70

happened to her was just a dream. Her knowledge of martial arts, lasso swinging, and firearms was a silly what if. Her chase with the police and the very dramatic wrecking of her car never happened. Kidnapping Chad Singer and him turning into a black-eyed monster was nothing more than an unconscious acid trip.

Imagination was incredible.

For a moment, Rosemary truly thought it was all real.

But when the throes of slumber were gone, bright lights flashed before her eyes. It hurt to look at the luminance, and she instantly forced her eyes closed. A red sheen greeted the blonde from behind her eyelids. "*Ack*," she whined, trying to throw her hand up to shield her line of sight just enough for her to feel safe opening her eyes again; emphasis on the word *trying*.

Her hand wouldn't raise. No matter how much she strained, the arm simply wouldn't come up. Rosemary tried her other arm, only to meet the same conclusion. "W-Wha—"

A deep, masculine cough interrupted her. "Relax, dear," said an unmistakably British voice. "We injected you with a serum that causes sleep paralysis. Struggling won't get you anywhere."

Now the blonde was beginning to panic. The last thing she remembered was fighting with Chad Singer. Who was *this* guy? Where was she? Why did he have a serum that causes sleep paralysis?!

"*W-Who are you?*" she shrieked with a trembling voice. "*Who are you people?! Where am I?!*"

The voice didn't respond to her, instead clearing his throat. "Rodrick, turn the lights down. Our guest is overwhelmed."

Rosemary shook, heart and mind racing. "*Help*! *Somebody help me*!"

A warm, coarse hand placed itself onto her right shoulder, making her jump. "You may open your eyes now, love."

The woman swallowed hard and shook her head. "N-No!"

"It's quite alright," the voice goaded. "I believe you'll find the sight before you pleasant, perhaps even titillating. Go on, open up."

Rosemary's bottom lip quivered. Did she dare? There was no telling what would be awaiting her on the other side. She held onto the darkness like a security blanket. Nothingness had to have been better than looking into the eyes of men who were possibly planning on killing her.

Alas, she knew she couldn't keep her eyes closed forever. Curiosity would eventually overcome her. Not to mention autopilot controlling her eyelids, should she somehow fall back asleep. So with a defeated sigh, Rosemary slowly opened her eyes.

Rodrick indeed turned the lights down. Now the room was mostly shrouded in darkness, save for the spotlight above her. She was clearly laying on some hard surface, but the numbness in her body made it impossible to feel anything. And unexpectedly, meeting her gaze was a beautiful Caucasian man with a strong jawline.

He had hazel eyes with short sandy blonde hair. He was shirtless and jean-clad, sporting a chiseled four-pack. She soon learned he was the owner of the British accent. Honestly, that fact on top of an already fuckable body just made her lust for him even greater.

Funny, she'd never had a kidnapping kink.

Guess it was as good a time as any to develop one.

"Are you hurt?" he asked. Appearing out from behind him was another shirtless hunk with a nice set of abs. This guy had long chestnut brown hair with matching eyes. This must've been Rodrick.

"*Bonjour*," he greeted with a thick French accent. "Zis must be quite ze shock for you."

Rosemary tried not to salivate.

If she knew being kidnapped would reward her with such luscious eye-candy, she would've posted her address on message boards and anxiously waited for the first creep to come pick her up.

Rodrick looked up past Rosemary's head, giving her the full view of his sexy Adam's apple. "You could've been a bit more delicate with ze lady, Chad."

The blonde's eyes widened. "*Chad*?!" She tried to look up at the dark-skinned man, but her neck could only bend back so far while laying down.

"She knows far too much," he explained. "It's only a matter of time until she unearths the details behind the grand scheme."

Having not heard what he said, Rosemary growled. "How are you still alive?! I shot you with a fucking *grenade launcher*!"

The former boss man chuckled darkly. "It takes more than firepower to kill us."

Suddenly, and much to Rosemary's befuddlement, more shirtless men appeared from the shadows. Before she knew it, the warm presence of more men behind her made itself known. The blonde was surrounded, not another woman in sight. Some men were white, some were black. There were also indigenous men and Hispanic men. There were even Middle-Easterners and Asians.

And they were all *hot.*

Any dick-loving man or woman would have begged to be in Rosemary's shoes at that moment.

"*Wow!*" she squealed, all anxious now thrown out the window. "Which one of you is going first? My body is *ready.*"

An Asian man to her left chuckled. "Eager beaver, isn't she?" He looked down at her and ran a hand up her thigh. "You're the best example of why our plan is so perfect."

The blonde cocked an eyebrow. "Plan? What are you talking about? Who are you guys, even? A troupe of sex gods?"

One Hispanic man with pierced nipples reached down and caressed her cheek. "We're the Born."

"Pablo, *no,*" Chad hissed.

However, the gentle Pablo shook his head defiantly. "No nothing. She's made it this far, and I think the charade has gone on for far longer than it's needed to," he looked back down at Rosemary and smiled. "We're the children who watch over your species, Senorita. We are the above, the pharaohs, the kings, and the princes. We are born from the seeds of Yahweh and Satan," Pablo took the blonde's numb hand and raised it to his mouth, planting a soft kiss on the knuckle. "*We are what you call the overlords of space and time.*"

Rosemary squealed loudly. She was positively glowing. Whatever fear she had experienced beforehand had dissipated. Her truths were truths all along! She wasn't lying at all! If she weren't afflicted with sleep paralysis, she'd hop off the slab and break into the dance. Then she'd send a mass spam text of middle finger emojis to everyone she'd ever met.

Aliens!

Real, honest to God, *aliens*!

Alas, her heart rate transitioned from a pleasant pump-up to a heavy yet speedy pound. Her enthusiasm was noted, but there was still a gigantic elephant in the room. She'd hate herself if she didn't investigate that elephant thoroughly. And so, she opened her mouth to speak.

"So...what exactly *is* the grand scheme? People on Earth sort of think I'm crazy, so I'd like some kind of credibility when arguing my points against them."

Chad growled, stepping in front of the blonde so he was looking down at her. His eyes had turned back into their beautiful browns. "Explaining our plans defeats the very purpose of what we're trying to accomplish!"

The Asian man from earlier touched the former boss man's bare shoulder. "Chad, let it go."

"*No!*" the dark-skinned man shouted. "Why can't we just kill her?!"

Even though his desire to murder wasn't surprising to the blonde at this point, his words still stabbed her directly into the heart. She'd pined and longed for that man for a long time. She thought he really liked her, but he was just leading her on. Being abducted by aliens aside, *that* was the hardest pill to swallow out of the whole bottle.

"She's already planted a seed," Rodrick argued. "Seeds grow into trees. Killing ze seed is pointless, as it's already grown roots. What would it hurt to water ze seed one last time?"

Rosemary licked her bottom lip. "I mean, I've heard theories, but a theory isn't as nice as a fact."

Chad groaned, looking back at the blonde woman. "Isn't it obvious, Rosemary? Look all around you! What do you see?"

The eccentric blonde offered a playful wink at her former boss. "A bunch of really attractive men."

"*Precisely*," the unnamed British man said with a nod. "The best and easiest way for mother and father's message to be spread isn't through exposé podcasts. It's through frivolous entertainment mediums."

Rosemary squinted. "I don't follow."

"Think of it this way," Pablo intervened. "The most popular genre of media is romance. Books, movies, even music; it's everywhere. Mother and Father want everyone to love each other, so what better way than to send us to make some lonely housewives feel loved or some closeted homosexual men feel accepted?"

The British man nodded. "We can be gentle and loving, or we can be haughty and mean-spirited. Every love story has its own flavor. Some are mutual conquests; others are unrequited tragedies. But it's better to have loved and lost than to have never loved at all."

Rosemary tried to follow along but was finding herself stumped. "Does that mean there's women here, too? Women who are alien agents?"

"Not quite," Chad chimed in. "Mother is the only female alien in all of existence. We're all men."

"*Huh*?" the blonde squawked. "But the pharaohs, including the women, were all sent from the sky!"

"There were never any women pharaohs," Chad commented. "Whatever history book told you that is lying."

Rosemary huffed, annoyed. "*Okay*. Then answer me this: if you're all hot men trying to seduce lonely men and women, what about lesbians? They aren't attracted to men at all."

Chad snorted. "Lesbians aren't real, Rosemary."

The blonde growled. "Yes they are!"

"*No*," the former boss argued, raising his voice. "They are *not*."

"Quite true," the British man added quickly. "They are within the same figment of imagination that houses the Easter Bunny and Santa Claus."

The woman stared blankly at the aliens for a moment before eventually succumbing to defeat with a deep sigh. "I'm learning a lot more than I thought I would."

"Indeed," said the unnamed Asian man who touched her. "So now you understand why we had to silence you?"

Rosemary shook her head. "No, I don't. How are my podcasts diverting attention away from romantic books and movies? I'm just one woman with one podcast."

Soon, a rugged shirtless fellow with a beard and short black hair stepped forward, his thumbs resting in his belt loops. "Darlin'," he greeted with a Texan accent. "You ain't the only one that's bin talkin' bout us; yer just the one who knew the most. But if yer show was bigger, we'd be screwed. We hadda get involved!"

The blonde woman eyeballed the hunk and let the gears in her head spin. Aliens and romance are somehow synonymous with each other. The men are infesting the media to make people fall in love. But by being a sexless scrub who obsesses over ancient alien lore, Rosemary is jeopardizing their plans by bringing awareness to their ingenious plan. "I understand now!" the blonde exclaimed.

Chad frowned. "So you do. Now that you've figured everything out, we have no choice but to erase all of Mother and Father's hard work."

Rosemary's eyes widened. "Wait, no!"

The men's eyes all turned solid black and their breathing echoing from the ceiling. Colorful lights began to flash like Fourth of July fireworks popping in the sky. The room was still a shadow, but she could now see more than just the men. The particular room they were in was hollow, but the steel texture of the walls told her it was the brig.

"Send nukes to Earth," Rodrick commanded, his voice blasting all around the room. "Three, two, one."

Rosemary tried to protest, but she was too late.

Her screams weren't capable of washing out the cataclysmic explosion.

12

A Perfect Storm

Rosemary stood in the observation deck, looking out the window with her arms crossed. Many children had dreams of going into space. They wanted to go to the Moon, Mars, Jupiter, and Saturn. They wanted to ride in spaceships. They wanted to meet aliens.

She used to be one of those kids. And because her dream came true, nobody else would follow in her footsteps. No more children would dream of space and aliens. Billions of years of history and hard work were gone all because she had a big, fat mouth.

From a distance, Rosemary couldn't tell what Earth's debris was and what were stars. She knew the large gaping hole beside the Moon and Sun was where her home used to be. The larger rocks were obvious to spot, but she dared not look too long; she didn't want to see any bodies floating in zero gravity space.

It was funny in a sickening, morbid sense. Rosemary had always hated people and the way the world worked. Politicians and the military were both killing the planet slowly and painfully. The creation of the atomic bomb set the planet en route to its destruction. But nobody, not the politicians or warmongers or anyone for that matter, could've possibly guessed the end of the world would come from a young woman asking too many questions.

Maybe she took it all for granted.

Maybe it was better this way.

There was no way of knowing.

That scared the blonde beyond measure.

Rosemary found herself tearing up at the memories of her childhood. Eating barbeque with her mom and pop. Playing with the family dog, Spot. Making her first friend in fifth grade.

All of them were dead now.

Her beloved Roswell was, too.

As she sobbed, the door behind her slid open. She didn't look behind her, but the reflection in the window told her all she needed to know. "Leave me alone, Chad."

Presenting with human eyes, the dark-skinned man sighed. "I get it. I really do. It sucks to lose your home."

Rosemary glared at his reflection and swung around. "*Shut the fuck up,*" she ordered with a scowl. "You know *nothing.*"

The former boss snorted. "Do I, now? I know more than you do. I'm *ancient.* So, you should probably guess that I've experienced a tragedy of this magnitude."

The eccentric blonde tilted her head to the side. "Have you really?"

Chad looked into her eyes for a moment. His brown eyes burned into her soul. But then he burst out into laughter. "*No!* Of course not! Are you fucking stupid?"

The woman didn't react, instead just looking mindlessly down at the floor. She felt broken. Everything she'd ever known was the truth, yes. But her overwhelming brain power got everyone killed. It was so hard being a monumentally important person.

"I'm *not* stupid," she murmured. "That's the problem."

Chad smirked, folding his arms. "Yes. Yes it *was* the problem. If you didn't focus so much on this, you'd still be on Earth. You'd be playing with your kitty, and then go on to play with the damn cat," he sighed. "But you know. I wasn't kidding when I said I was entranced by women with your aptitude for figuring shit out."

Rosemary looked at him. "Really?"

"Yes really," he confirmed. "You're crazy, but beautiful and smart. I admire you, and also fear you."

"*Fear me*," Rosemary repeated under her breath, before raising her voice. "That makes sense, after what's happened."

Chad smirked, offering her a wink. "My little angel of death, you are."

The blonde smiled, oddly finding comfort in his words. She was the only human remaining in the universe. She needed to repopulate another planet somewhere. And if she had to choose a mate, she'd rather not go for anyone else than the man who first unleashed her inner ravenous beast.

"Now that we're in a new life, why don't we try again? The two of us together, I mean."

The alien chuckled. "I'd like that."

He stepped up to her and pulled her in for a kiss. She feverishly held onto him, refusing to let go. Her grip grew tighter and tighter. "I love you, Chad Singer," she cried.

The syringe punctured her right ass cheek.

And his face began to fade to white.

www.ingramcontent.com/pod-product-compliance
Lightning Source LLC
Chambersburg PA
CBHW052203150726
48002CB00003B/1102